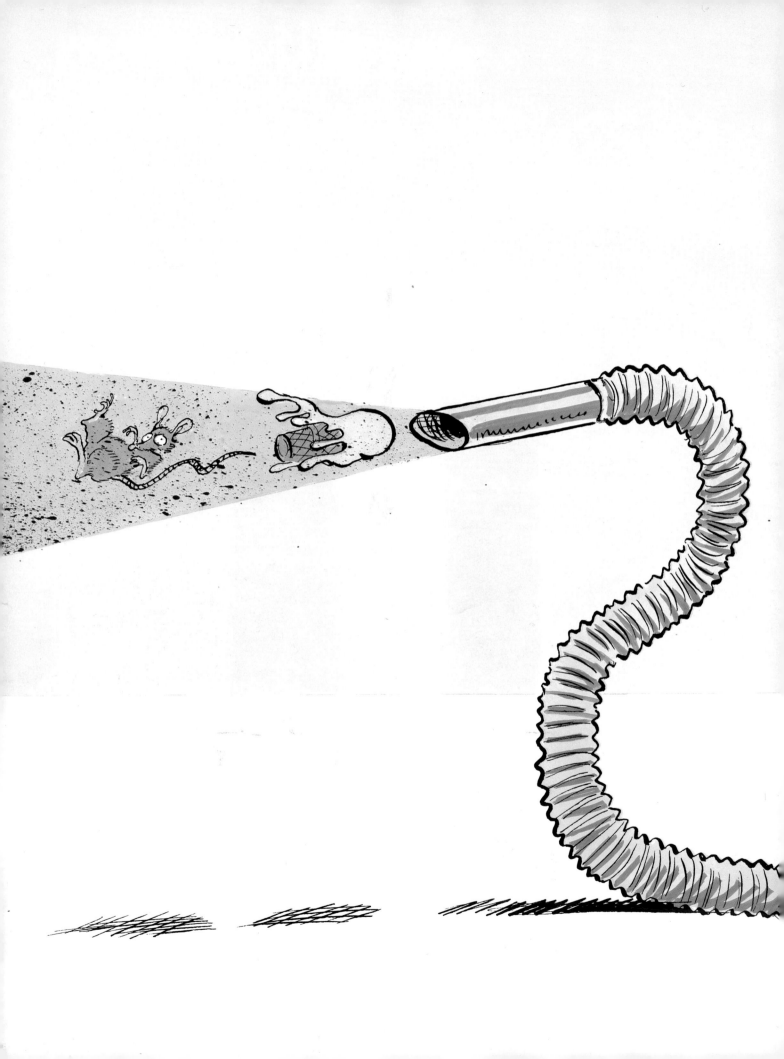

Hoover's Bride

written and illustrated by
David Small

Crown Publishers, Inc. New York

For Sarah

with special thanks to Ted Schnur

Published by Crown Publishers, Inc., a Random House company,
201 East 50th Street, New York, New York 10022

CROWN is a trademark of Crown Publishers, Inc.

Manufactured in Singapore

Library of Congress Cataloging-in-Publication Data
Small, David. 1945-
Hoover's bride / by David Small.
p. cm.
Summary: Hoover's house is overrun with dust until he marries a vacuum cleaner, but he soon discovers that humans and appliances are not meant to wed.
[1. Vacuum cleaners—Fiction. 2. Marriage—Fiction. 3. Stories in rhyme.
4. Humorous stories.] I. Title.
PZ8.3.S634Ho   1995
[E]—dc20   94-43856

ISBN 0-517-59707-1 (trade)
0-517-59708-X (lib. bdg.)

10 9 8 7 6 5 4 3

*H*oover's old house was in need of repairs,
With its broken-out windows and broken-down stairs.
The grass in the yard, never cut, sprouted wildly.
To call it a jungle was putting it mildly.

The dust trickled down in delicate rills,
But soon mounted up into generous hills.
While Hoover relaxed with the TV cartoons,
Little by little, those hills became dunes.

Then one afternoon, at a quarter to five,

A falling dust mote caused a major landslide.

Hanging his head, his face crimson with shame,

Hoover knew he had no one but Hoover to blame.

KLIK
- KLIK
- KLIK

Covered with dust from his shoes to his hair,

He staggered out, panting and gasping for air.

While over the roof hung an ominous cloud,

Below, on the sidewalk, collected a crowd.

A lady, in unconcealed tones of disgust, said,
    "It seems to have been a while, sir, since you've dusted.

"Now here's a machine that will make it so easy
    To clean up your house and to make it less sleazy.
"It's a vacuum machine that will pick up your dirt.
    See? It cleans off the mat and the front of your shirt . . .

"The foyer, the hallway, the carpet, the stair.
   Just look at the stuff that was buried in there."

Reformed, Hoover fell to the floor on his knees.
   "I'm a new man!" he cried. "Will you marry me? Please?"
Simpered the lady, "You flatter me, sir!"
   "I didn't mean *you*," Hoover said. "I meant *her*—
That vision of beauty so bright and pristine . . .

That utterly marvelous vacuum machine!"

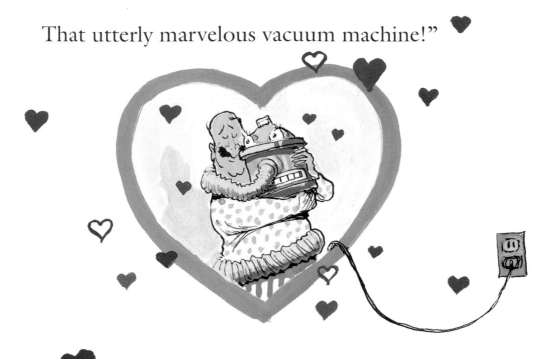

Her name was Elektra. He bought her a ring—
And he didn't buy her just any old thing.
A grapefruit-size diamond was what Hoover chose
In a size that would fit on the end of her hose.

Said the priest, "While this seems like the strangest alliance,
I now pronounce you Man and Appliance."
Stepping outside, they were pelted with rice,
But they swept up the steps, leaving everything nice.

Next, the reception—a gala affair.

    Hoover and bride—an adorable pair.

With everyone dancing and nobody looking,

    Elektra rolled over to sample the cooking.

After salad, spaghetti, a cheese-and-nut ball,

    A quick-witted chef pulled her plug from the wall.

Their honeymoon started on notes of unease:
Elektra inhaled a guest's prize Pekinese.

Thank heaven the animal caused her to wheeze,
  And she snorted it out with a bad-mannered sneeze.

On the boardwalk, Hoover developed the notion
They needed a much better view of the ocean.
So using an outlet within easy reach . . .

They quickly, completely, leveled the beach.

After brushing his teeth and washing his face,
　And tucking Elektra into her case,
Hoover turned out the light and was starting to snore
　When a horrid commotion was heard from next door.

A thunderous noise shook the bed—shook the wall!
Hoover threw on his robe and dashed into the hall.

He knocked. The door opened. "Pardon me," Hoover said.
"Will you please quiet down? We have just gone to bed."

The lady said, "Truly, I'm sorry for that,
   My husband and I were just having a chat."
"If you and your husband require a discussion,
   Then what is the meaning of all this percussion?"
"My husband," she said, "cannot make his voice lower.
   He happens to be a power lawn mower."

"Ah, yes!" Hoover took a much friendlier tone.
"These machines we adore have minds of their own!
Forgive me if seeds of dissension I've sown.
I'll go now and leave you two lovebirds alone."

Hoover made the discovery by dawn's early light:
His new bride had disappeared during the night.
Though they searched the hotel from the roof to the ground,
Not a trace of a wheel mark or cord could be found.

Hoover said, "If not cleaned up, a mess simply worsens.
I'm off to the Bureau of Missing Persons!"

The officer said, "Now, have I got this straight?
    She's shaped like a bucket...and trimmed in chrome plate?
Cute little wheels? A seven-foot nose?
    (Though some people say that it's really a hose)—?"

Then who should appear but Room Two-Fifty-Two!
   "This is surprising! My husband's gone, too!
I parked him last evening outside on the lawn,
   But went down this morning and found he was gone.
I've searched every place. Where, oh, where can he be?"
   Hoover said, "Dear, forget him. Have dinner with *me!*"

Back at the restaurant, over champagne,
A starry-eyed Hoover proposed once again.

Said the judge, "While it's true that the law is quite hazy,
In this case it's clear: your weddings were crazy.
Women and men should not marry machines!
It is simply not done! No, no, no! By no means!"

So they married, and now, whatever the weather,
Hoover and bride are happy together.
She loves to mow, while his bliss is to clean.
As for those two naughty missing machines . . .

A mile and a half was as far as they got.

They're rusting for now in a city junk lot.

They learned that it's good to have humans aboard

When you run out of gas, or run out of cord.

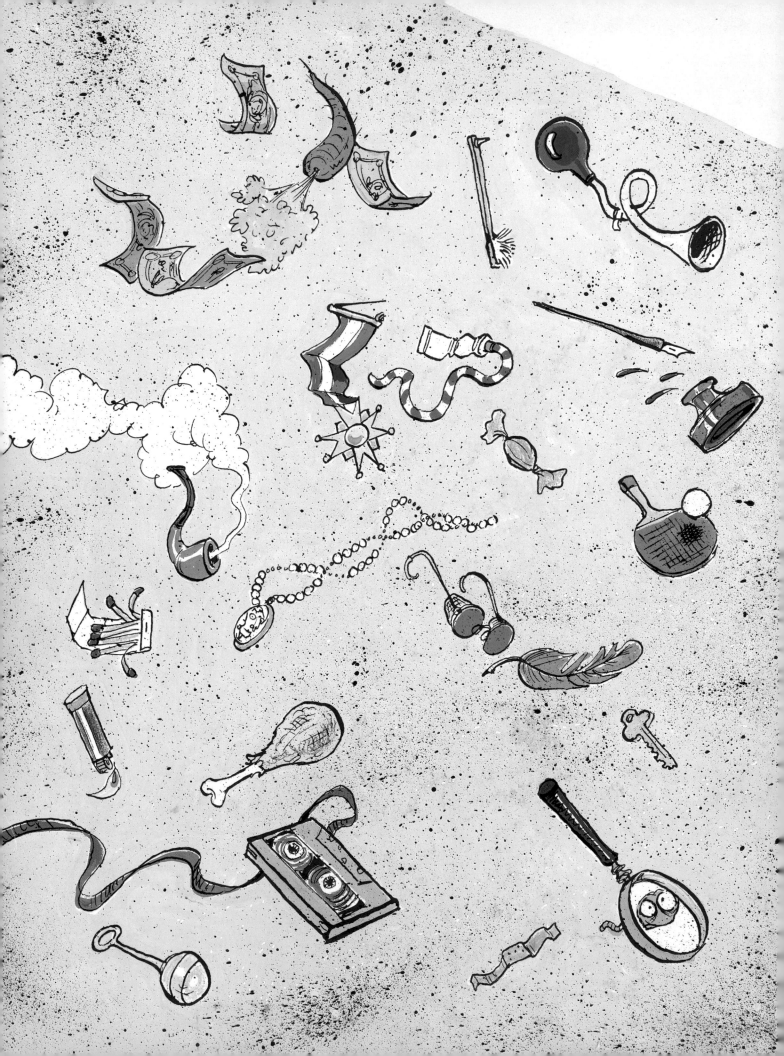